# BOGEYMEN

## Jan Needle

*Illustrated by Liz Tofts*

André Deutsch Children's Books

Scholastic Children's Books,
Scholastic Publications Ltd,
7–9 Pratt Street, London NW1 0AE, UK

Scholastic Inc.,
730 Broadway, New York, NY 10003, USA

Scholastic Canada Ltd,
123 Newkirk Road, Richmond Hill,
Ontario, Canada L4C 3G5

Ashton Scholastic Pty Ltd,
PO Box 579, Gosford, New South Wales,
Australia

Ashton Scholastic Ltd,
Private Bag 1, Penrose, Auckland,
New Zealand

First published in the UK by Scholastic Publications Ltd, 1992

Text Copyright © 1992 by Jan Needle

Illustrations Copyright © 1992 by Liz Tofts

ISBN 0 590 54015 7

Typeset by Wyvern Typesetting Ltd, Bristol, UK
Printed in Great Britain by The Bath Press, Avon

*For Chris*
*(And Percy, naturally)*

# CHAPTER ONE

"Have you ever had the feeling that you're wasting time?" said Snatch Pearson. "You know, not just letting it go by, or passing it, but really, really wasting it?"

He was sitting at the top of a high wall of crumbling brick, and a light, warm wind was blowing through his hair. Next to him a girl was sitting, in jeans and a tee shirt. She was kicking her heels against the brickwork. Bolly Fisher.

"Well," she said. "What do you expect to do in this dump? See a bank robbery? Watch Concorde crash into a haystack? I saw a weasel get run over once. When I was seven. That was the high point of my life."

Snatch did not laugh. He was busy working a piece of brick free from the rotted cement. He was going to throw it at Bolly's little brother, Cy, who was playing with a pile of sand down in the builders yard. He had thrown several pieces in the past half-hour. No one minded.

The day was warm, and very quiet. One of those country days where everything seemed to have slowed down, even planes. The noise the jets made, far away, was dull and lazy, not harsh and deafening as it should have been. Since they had arrived to do their watching, they had counted seven cars along the road. Seven. In nearly two hours. As Snatch had said not once but several times – it was pathetic.

The small brick missile freed at last, Snatch eyed up Cy's blond head. He had built an elaborate roadway system in the yellow sand, and he was pushing a couple of toy cars around it. Behind a sand dune, a Lego pirate with a long brown pistol waited, a villain from another century. Cy was only nine.

"Nothing ever happens in this dump," said Bolly Fisher. "That's the simple truth of it. Don't get him on the head, will you? He'll only cry. He makes me clean the snot up."

The missile was already in the air. It came down from the wall in a gentle arc, over two burst bags of cement that damp had long since turned to solid stone. It landed neatly on the pirate, squashing him into the dune. Cy grinned.

"H-bomb," he said. "Good that. Shall I set them up in a line so we can all chuck things? That'd be all right!"

The two older children made faces.

"Oh," said Snatch. "I don't think I could stand all the excitement, Cy . . ."

Behind them, they heard panting. Bolly glanced over her shoulder. There was an alleyway along the backs of all the terrace gardens, ending in the wall that she and Snatch were sitting on. Martin Turner was running down it, with a two-litre bottle of cola jigging in his hands. Not Coke or Pepsi, the cheapie stuff the little shop sold. He was sweating.

"Chee, it's hot. This was in the fridge, it was cold when I bought it. It's like soup now. Disgusting."

The wall was high, so Snatch leaned downwards as Martin stretched up. The bottle changed hands, then Martin scrambled carefully upwards. Cy had dislodged a loose brick once, and it had fallen on his head, causing much blood to flow, and tears. Martin was swinging his legs into place as Snatch, then Bolly, swigged. He held his hand out for the bottle.

"Any sign of them?" asked Bolly. There was a brown stain on her mouth from the cheap cola. Her hands were too dirty to wipe it off.

"Nah," replied Martin. "Nothing. It's as if the whole world's died out there. I saw a hedgehog on the main road. Safe as anything."

"Why did the hedgehog cross the road?" said Snatch,

automatically. "It was looking for a flat."

"That can't be right," said Bolly. "It's not even funny."

"I think it's right," said Snatch. "Maybe it should be a flatmate. Yeah, that's it."

"The tar was boiling," said Martin. "It was coming up in bubbles. It's a wonder the hedgehog wasn't standing on its tiptoes."

"I wonder where they are, though," said Snatch. "Maybe they're doing it on purpose, just to bore us. Maybe it's a conspiracy. Maybe they're not coming after all."

"Oh they'll come," said Martin. "They're moving in today, my mum says. You know her – she knows everything."

Bolly laughed.

"Except that you're up here. Going against your word. Mummy's boy."

"Get knotted, you. You'd've promised too if you'd been made to. You just don't live practically next door, that's all, I bet your mum and dad don't even know you come here."

The talking fizzled out, and they sat baking quietly. The cola bottle was handed round again, and Cy stretched up for his share. Snatch – in a friendly way – rubbed his trainer in the tousled hair, which was already full of sand. Bolly checked her watch from time to time.

The fun, thought Martin Turner, had gone out of it since Old Man Quigley had died. Although they were forbidden, still, to climb the wall or jump down into the untidy yard and wander, there wasn't much sense of danger when you knew he wasn't there to fly out and hit you with a stick. It was a weird way to miss somebody, but they did. Little bent old swine.

"D'you remember that time he got Bolly by the hair?" he said, to no one in particular. "Old Man Quigley? You had pigtails then, Bol. Is that why you cut them off?"

"I pushed the water barrel over," said Snatch. "It went all over those stinky old plimsolls he had on. All up his legs. He went hairless."

"Sir Galahad," said Bolly, sarcastically. "You saved my life."

"Yeah," responded Snatch. "Stupid, isn't it? Saving the dragon instead of a fair maiden!"

"I wish he hadn't died," said Martin. "It's horrible to think about it, isn't it? Him lying there in that old kitchen, all on his tod. Three days, they reckon, before anyone even knew. He might have been alive for hours. Days. That's horrible."

Cy had left his sand. He was gazing up at them.

"We could've come in while he was lying there," he said. "We could've played while he was dying. Gruesome."

"Only we didn't," said Martin. "Shut it, Cy."

"All on his tod," said Bolly. "It's funny you should say that, Martin. Tod's German for dead. That's incredible."

"Yeah," muttered her little brother. "Incredibly boring, eh Martin? Show-off."

"The really horrible thing," Snatch put in, "is that it spoiled it. I mean, look at it now. We could do anything we liked. We could go in any of the sheds, we could nick anything, we could chuck wallbricks through his windows if we wanted. We could wreck the place. No point."

"But we wouldn't want to, anyway," said Bolly, sanctimoniously. "We never did anything really bad, did we? I mean, we never took anything valuable, did we?"

Snatch jeered, but it was largely true. Old Man Quigley only dealt in junk, and they had only removed the most useless stuff from time to time, stuff nobody would have paid for. Not that anybody ever paid, come to that, thought

Martin. Old Man Quigley hadn't had a proper customer for years. The memory of taking things still worried him, however. Sometimes.

"We put it back, in any case," he said. "Some of the junk, after we'd messed about with it, we chucked it back, didn't we? He never knew the difference. He had no idea what he had and what he didn't have. He was eccentric, my mum says."

They could all agree with that. Old Man Quigley was called such things by all their parents. He was a "funny old chap", a "real odd fellow", a "recluse". The kids had actually gone to his funeral – although only secretly, they had not been invited or anything like that. They had hidden in the bushes in the churchyard and watched him buried by the vicar and some men they didn't recognise whom Bolly's mother later said worked for the council and got paid to bury people no one knew. It was not a proper funeral, there were no ladies in black dresses or weeping relatives. Old Man Quigley had left the town as friendless as he'd lived in it.

"Yeah," said Snatch. "He was a weirdo, no mistake. I bet the new ones won't be anything like as good. I bet if we try trespassing they'll just call the police and that'll be that. They'll tell the headmaster and we'll be banned. Boring."

Cy Fisher, already bored by all the talk, had wandered to

the opposite side of the yard. He came scuttling back wide-eyed.

"There's a lorry coming! It must be them! Quick! Help me up! Listen!"

They did not have to strain their ears. Before they could see the lorry, before they could even catch its engine, they could hear music. It was insistent music with a thumping beat. They stared at each other.

Then Snatch swung his legs sideways and dropped back over the wall into the alleyway outside the yard. Cy gave a shriek.

"Help me! Don't leave me here!"

Bolly and Martin stretched over to grab his hands. As they did so, the cola bottle rolled then fell.

"Get the coke!"

"No, leave it!"

"Pull me up! *Quick!*"

Martin, glancing up, saw the lorry stop outside the gates, which were made of slatted wood that you could see through. It was a small lorry, a pick-up, blue and rust-coloured. The rocking music was very loud.

Cy's sharp fingernails dug into his wrist. The little boy's face was shocked and sweaty, his eyes imploring. Bolly and Martin threw their weight backwards and hauled him up the wall.

"The bricks will fall," wailed Cy, showing the gappy teeth the Fishers were well known for. "They'll smash my head in!"

"Shut up, you wimp," snapped Bolly. Beside her, Snatch's head appeared, grinning devilishly.

"Leave him!" he said. "Leave him to the wolves! Hey, where's the drink?"

Too late for that. As Cy rolled over the top of the wall and Martin and Bolly began to scramble after him, the gates were rattled.

"Down!" said Snatch. "Before they clock us!"

Then his mouth hung open for an instant. His eyes widened like a cartoon boy's.

Before Martin's head dropped below the top of the wall he had registered the same shock. The gates had parted in the middle and two faces had appeared. Big faces, long and wide and shining in the heat. There were smiles on them, broad smiles of happiness.

But they were black.

# CHAPTER TWO

Despite his smallness, when his feet hit the ground Cy left the others standing, he put his head down and *ran*. They were almost at the far end of the alleyway before Snatch caught and overtook him, shoving him to one side like a ruthless runner in the Olympics. But Cy still made it second to the gap.

By the time Martin reached the spot and turned, Snatch was well across the overgrown garden, with Cy hard on his heels. Martin, pausing for a split second to get the entry angle right, was knocked into by Bolly.

"They were coming for the wall!" she panted. "They were coming!"

Her face was frantic as she pushed past him, and Martin, glancing back, caught a movement in the shadows at the far end of the alleyway. She was right!

The entrance to their hideout was narrow, a piece of brick wall that had fallen and been blocked with junk ages ago. He squeezed through, smelling the rank smell of weeds and rubble and damp mattresses. Too slow, too slow! Bolly was already at the boarded-up back door. He saw her push the plank aside and wriggle through. She had gained fifteen metres on him, the length of what had once been the back garden of the corner shop, long derelict. He paused to catch his breath. At least he could stand upright safely here. Even from his own bedroom, just down the row, you could not see into this high-walled space. But alone, he was not safe. United, they might stand! He headed for the door, his heart still thumping painfully. Inside, maybe, there'd be a bit of peace and sanity.

At the bottom of the twisted, floppy staircase leading to the attic that they used, it appeared that he'd been wrong. He could hear raised voices, Snatch shouting angrily, Cy whining. It was mixed with the mighty clattering of Bolly's feet as she reached the top. She always went up the ruined stairs as if they were quite safe, and mocked Martin for his caution. He touched the banister, still shaking from her run. One day, he knew, the staircase would fall down on them, the whole lot. In the meantime, he was mocked . . .

By the time he reached the attic, having gone much faster

than he usually dared, the mood had changed. Cy was crying, but the whine had been replaced with furious defiance.

"But what if they're following?" he was shouting. "What if they saw us?"

"I'm telling you," Snatch Pearson shouted back. "They didn't see! They'd never find us anyway, would they?"

"Shut up!" yelled Martin, adding to the clamour. "I saw them in the alleyway! Shut up!"

For an instant there was silence, which Cy destroyed with a rising wail. His sister darted at him like an angry sheepdog, threatening his face. He tried to stop, but the bubblings continued.

Snatch was irritable.

"You didn't see a thing, Martin," he said. "You're as bad as Cy, you are. I'm telling you, they didn't see us, OK? If they knew where we were we'd've heard them now, wouldn't we? Even over Blubberguts. Shut it, Cy! Listen!"

Cy spluttered to a stop. They listened. There was nothing. Just the buzzing of a fly in the hot attic, trapped behind a window.

It made sense. The gap they'd come through in the outside wall would not be easily spotted if you did not know it. The four of them were the only people in the area, they were pretty certain, who knew you could get into the old shop at all. It was on the opposite end of the terrace to Old Man Quigley's yard, and it was boarded front and back, with red and white danger warnings. There had been coalmines in the area in the old days, and the corner shop's foundations had slipped.

"See?" said Snatch. "Nothing. See?"

"But I saw them," said Cy, rebelliously. "I thought they were coming through the gates at us."

"You're always seeing things," said Snatch. "You ought

to see a doctor some day. You're a head case."

They laughed, and even Cy raised a smile, reluctantly. Bolly threw herself onto a dusty mattress in a patch of sunshine from the skylight. She shook her head.

"Who'd have thought it, though," she said. "Old Man Quigley'll be turning in his grave. *Blacks*."

"Yeah," said Cy, morosely. "That's the end of playing in the builders yard, isn't it? They'd murder us. They'd have us in the pot for supper."

Martin was about to laugh. But Snatch and Bolly, he saw, were nodding sombrely.

Apparently, they agreed.

# CHAPTER THREE

Martin Turner, at twelve years old, had never seen a black man face to face. Neither, he suspected, had any of his friends.

At school, a couple of the teachers made quite a thing about the "coloured population", and he knew all about the "multi-racial society" they lived in. The trouble was, there weren't any in their town, and there weren't any in their school. Maybe black people didn't go in for farming.

They did in Africa, obviously. There were pictures on the classroom wall of people with few clothes on and strange, skinny cows with humps on their backs. There were pictures of kids in India, as well, pumping water up in dry and dusty landscapes. But in Britain, Martin guessed, black people – and brown – lived in the big towns, or in

London.

"They don't eat people, fool," he said to Cy. "You watch *Grange Hill*, don't you? When did one of the black kids ever get to cook a teacher?!"

"That's on TV," said Cy. "That's the government. You can't show them doing bad things on the telly, it's against the law."

This was so crazy that Martin gaped. Bolly, however, was nodding vigorously.

"That's right," she said. "The telly people have got to show them looking good, or they go to prison. There's far too many of them, see, that's the trouble. They're taking over from the white people, and it's against the law to say so."

"But why?" said Martin. "And if there's too many of them, why don't we see them round here?"

Snatch hooted. He was the oldest, and pretty smart. Martin had badly wanted him on his side.

"They've just arrived!" he said. "Nice one, Martin! Come on, stop arguing. I want to have a look."

Bolly had already started pushing a rickety armchair into position underneath the dormer skylight. Now Snatch tried to shove her to one side. They struggled violently for several seconds.

Martin felt oppressed. The air in the attic was heavy, the

sweet smell of hay from outside mixed with the sharper, sour smell of rotting furniture and damp soot from the fireplace. He knew nothing about black people, but he knew he was not about to get eaten. He could imagine how his dad would respond to the idea.

Snatch had won the fight, as always, and was clambering up the shaky chair-back. The window was built into the roof, and if you jammed yourself into the dormer and leaned out, you could get a good sight for miles across the countryside, as well as down the back of the terrace and one side of the village. Snatch got his elbows safely locked in position and let his legs swing free.

"There's two of them!" he shouted.

"Shush!" said Bolly, nervously. "They'll hear you!"

"Get your head in," said Martin. "What did you say?"

Snatch drew his head back through the window frame, being careful not to slice it off on the jagged broken glass.

"Two of them," he repeated. "Big black devils! They're enormous, honestly, like giants. There's a woman with a baby, too. Can't you hear the music?"

It drifted in, sometimes louder on the light, fitful wind. It was black music, thumping, hard. They did not like it.

"Course we can," said Bolly. "We're not deaf, you know. Come on, Snatch! Let's have a dekko."

"Hold the chair, I'm coming down."

The thin legs felt about until his trainers found the chair-back. Snatch glanced, assessed, balanced, then jumped onto the mattress on the floor. A cloud of dust flew into the air, dancing in the shafts of sunlight.

"There you go, Martin," he said. "You next."

Bolly glared at him, but without someone to hold the chair she could not safely do the climb. Snatch liked to make it known he was the boss. Martin, though, shook his head.

"Go on, Boll," he said, holding the chair for her. "I'll see them soon enough in any case, won't I? They're practically next-door neighbours."

Bolly giggled.

"Yeah. They'll be able to have you over for Sunday dinner. You'll be the roast!"

The chair wobbled as she climbed. He was tempted to let go.

"Give over, Boll," he said, uncomfortably. "They're only people."

"No, honestly," said Snatch. "You'd look quite good with an apple in your gob. Or some other useful orifice!"

"They would eat you," Cy said, seriously. "They drink blood, my dad says so."

"Get off!" said Martin. "That's ridiculous!"

"They do! They do! Our dad's been, they kill chickens!

Drink their blood!"

"Oh, cut it out," snapped Martin. "You're just stupid. Been where?"

Cy looked confused. His face was spectacularly dirty, a mixture of sand and soil and tears and cola stains.

"Oh, I dunno. That place in geography. When he had that big win. He was nearly there a whole fortnight."

Bolly, half in and half out of the window, peered down.

"Jamaica," she said. "He's right, you know, Martin. He wouldn't take Mum with him because he said it was too dangerous. They live on rum, and that. They're wild. Berserkers."

"They cut off chickens' heads in the market," said Cy. "Dad *saw* them. They drink the blood, all warm."

Snatch made a clutching monsters' claws with his hands and went at Cy, who ran across the attic, yelling.

"They up-end them like a milk bottle and drink it from the neck!" he said. "Just like I'm going to do to you, Cy. Come here! It's drinkie-time!"

"They're in!" squeaked Bolly, from above. "I can see their little lorry coming through the gates. Gaw, it isn't half a wreck. It's destitute. There's another one! A skinny bloke! He's got a tea cosy on his head!"

Snatch dropped Cy onto the floor and ran to the chair. He pulled at Bolly's dangling ankle.

"Come on! Down! Let's have another look! God, that's five of them in that poky little dump. Five! They must live like pigs."

Martin, without ever having had a proper sight of them, began to wish quite strongly that the blacks had never come. It was not just because Old Man Quigley's yard was finished, the fun killed off forever. It was for them as well.

He didn't know where they'd come from, but it seemed sad that they had not had the sense to stay at home. They were going to find trouble here, anyone could see that. As well as bringing it.

They could have saved themselves the bother.

# CHAPTER FOUR

That evening, Martin Turner rather hoped the subject of the new neighbours would be talked about. He had told his mother about them moving in when he had come in for tea, and the others had wandered home across the fields. She had not taken much notice.

"Yes, Mrs Fletcher mentioned it," she said. "She seemed to think there were a lot of them for one small house."

Martin held his breath. Surely his mum would not say they were like pigs?

"There's a little kid, apparently," she went on. "Just a babe in arms. That'll be a change after Mr Quigley, won't it? The Ancient Mariner!"

"Mariner?" said Martin. "That means a sailor, doesn't

it? Old Man Quigley wasn't a sailor, was he?"

She shook her head.

"It's a poem. About a really old bloke. One foot in the grave. He had a skinny arm and a glittering eye. Like Quigley."

"Quigley had two. Two arms, two eyes, one walking stick."

She tried to bat him with a floury hand.

"Idiot. They're black. Did you know?"

To his shame, Martin went bright red. His mother watched him, in that interested way she had. The red got brighter.

"Shut up!" he said. "Stop looking at me!"

"But I'm fascinated. What did I say? *Did* you know?"

Martin went up to his room, and his mother, who knew when to leave him, did not call after him or try to bring him down. Martin clattered about, switched on his computer, turned it off, took a jumper from a drawer then stuffed it back again. He was still blushing. It was as if his mother knew.

Knew what, though? About these thoughts? What thoughts? Martin went into the bathroom and rinsed his face in cold water. He pulled the chain to cover up his actions. He went downstairs.

"No," he said. "I didn't know for sure. We went playing

by the river so we didn't see them. Pete Williams told me he'd seen them. He said they were black but I thought he was kidding me. He was messing about."

He wondered why he'd told such an elaborate lie, and he felt sick about it. It was all so unnecessary.

"Oh," said his mother. "Well, I suppose round here it is quite funny, isn't it? Odd, anyway. Unusual. I don't think there are any more, are there? Black, or Asians? Even the chippy's run by an Englishman. Could you lay the table, love? Dad'll be here soon. He thought we might pop out for a drink later on. You wouldn't mind, would you?"

Martin did not, but as it happened, his father did not arrive. A few minutes later he rang up and told them to eat without him. He was a maintenance engineer at the feed-stuff plant, and a piece of machinery had broken down. When he did turn up, tired and drawn, he got out of his overalls, gobbled down his warmed-up meal, and put a pair of clean trousers and a jacket on for the pub. It was already nearly nine.

"Thanks, old son," he said. "You've got the number, haven't you, and Mrs Fletcher's there, if anything crops up. Don't stay awake for us."

After they had gone, Martin mooched. He liked being in the house alone, it meant his parents trusted him. When he'd been younger, Mrs Fletcher had come in from next

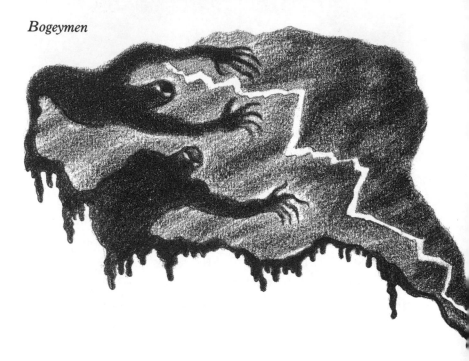

door, but now she sat by remote control. Tonight, though, he felt dissatisfied.

First he turned on the television, but it bored him, instantly. Then he went into the garden, and tried to find his frog in the half-dark. Over the high walls, to his surprise, he could still hear music, the same insistent, throbbing note he'd heard that afternoon. And laughter, hoots of it. Were they still outside? What were they doing?

It came into his mind to go into the alleyway through his back gate and get into the hideout. If he went up to the attic, he might be able to see them in the yard. But it was almost dark, and the stairs were dangerous. And who would hold the chair underneath the dormer? Maybe he should try and climb the wall? Put just his eyes over and peep? And be brained, he thought, when a brick fell off the top.

A large, cold raindrop hit his head. Half a second later another landed at his feet. There was a grumble of thunder and the drops fell faster. A rush of warm wind swept the small walled garden, carrying the cooler water. Martin jumped backwards for the door as the drops became a deluge. From the builders yard he thought he heard a whoop of wild elation. So far, he had seen no lightning.

When it started, it started with a vengeance. The sky was lit for what seemed like minutes at a time by barrages of flickering white and blue. Sometimes there were shorter flashes, followed by fractured bangs. Some cracks were ear-splitting, making him jump like a baby as they chased the hissing flash. The sky became ink-black, and when he turned them on, the kitchen lights flickered and dimmed. Even after his mother had phoned from the pub, Martin was half-afraid. He went up to his bedroom and climbed into bed, taking off only his trainers.

Reggae. That was the name of the fierce, unrelenting music. He imagined that he could hear it, in between the thunderous clashes of the storm. He must have drifted off as it moved away into the wild black night, but the fearful images remained. Black faces. Laughter. Teeth. He was pursued by bogeymen.

After what had been an age of torment, Martin woke up with a jerk. He lay sweating for a moment, on his back, his arms and legs spread out under the covers. His mouth was open, he was panting. He glanced at the display on his digital alarm.

It was ten to one, and the night was velvet black and cool. No wind, no rain, no thunder. But there was something.

Faintly it came to him, through the window he had closed against the storm.

It was the music.

# CHAPTER FIVE

Whatever tales Martin might believe about his new neighbours, terrific laziness could not be one of them.

For the first couple of days at school the week after they had moved in, Snatch, Bolly and Cy had kept up their interest – and interested other kids as well. Martin had been surrounded every playtime and asked for progress reports on how many chickens had been slaughtered, or other unimagined horrors revealed. Only the fact that his parents made him do his homework early every day, plus a week of drizzly, morbid weather, kept his friends at bay.

But they talked, and questioned, and bombarded him with information they thought he ought to know. Like the fact that yes, blacks did play music very loud, often all night, and that he would be lucky ever to get a good night's sleep again. And that they went in for big dogs that barked all night as well – when the music stopped – so he had another treat to look forward to. Also they cooked abysmal, smelly food, and threw the scraps over people's garden walls. Complaints would merely lead to bloodshed. Complaints about any of these things . . .

"What sort of food?" asked Martin. "I saw them coming back from the chippy the other night, in their truck. That's normal, isn't it?"

Cy and Bolly sneered.

"Cover," said Bolly. "Maybe they haven't got the gas switched on yet. Maybe they haven't sorted out the cooking pots. Curry, that's what they eat."

They were sitting in the playground eating sandwiches. A shower had just finished and the sun had come out like an opened oven door. The wall they perched on had steamed dry in seconds.

"Curry?" said Snatch. "That's Pakistanis, div. Curry's Indian, not black."

"West Indian!" said Bolly, triumphantly. "Jamaica's in the West Indies, isn't it? Even that old joke: 'My wife's gone to the West Ind—'"

"All right, all right. Don't go back in ancient history. I still say they don't eat curry. West India's got nothing to do with India."

"Curried goat," said Bolly. "You ask my dad. They sell it in the streets, you ask him. Every street corner in Jamaica, there's a geezer selling goat curry. And they keep them in their houses, bet me. Everyone keeps a goat in the back yard. And they kill them, it's their religion or something. They feed 'em up, then cut their throats one day. Shocking, it is. They run about, screeching and gurgling, then they turn them into curry."

"They put spells on people, too," said Cy. "It's true. The women. And the goats."

Snatch pushed him by the shoulder, in derision.

"Goats?! Goats put spells on people? Don't be stupid!"

"Don't you be stupid," said Cy, defiantly. "I didn't mean the goats, divvy. It's true the women put spells on you and it's true they kill the goats. You're the one that's stupid."

He was crouched ready to run, enjoying it. But Snatch could not be bothered with a chase.

"From what I've heard," he said, "they're too lazy to go round chasing goats. My old man says they're bone idle, all of them. They'd rather use the chippy, like Martin says."

The bell was going. End of intellectual chat, thought Martin. Thank God for that.

"Yeah," said Bolly, brushing the dampness off her skirt as she stood up. "Well, our dad's been there, hasn't he?

Our dad *knows*. They're lazy, but they curry goats as well. That's *fact*."

Martin had watched the men for three days now. He had watched them sweating. He had watched them working, half-murdering themselves, even in the muggy rain. They had filled five skips already, with Old Man Quigley's junk. They had torn down one old shed, they had dug up foundations, they had shifted tons of rubble. He had spied on them over the high wall.

"They're not lazy," he said, despite himself. "They work like . . . like lunatics."

Snatch shrieked with laughter.

"They work like niggers!" he said. "That's how they work! They work like niggers!"

"What are you blushing for?" asked Bolly. "Martin, you've gone all red!"

He did not know. For a moment, it felt absurdly as if Bolly were his mother, staring at him.

"Bell's gone," he muttered, and strode across the yard, head downwards, going fast.

"What a prat," he heard Snatch say. "Blushing like a girl."

"Watch it," said Bolly. "I don't blush."

"They are lunatics," said little Cy. "Our dad told us to keep away, didn't he, Boll? They put spells on people."

That evening, after he had done his homework, Martin put on his big padded jacket against the gently falling rain and slipped out, unseen by his mother, to the back alleyway. At the bottom of the end wall, he listened to the sounds. Reggae, reggae in the rain, and a rhythmic battering, like something being hit with heavy weights.

He had worked out a method now, of getting up and looking over without much chance of being seen. Runnels of water went down his neck as he inched his eyes above the top row of bricks. He blinked to clear his vision. The rhythmic blows did not falter.

They were over by the gates, and they were on boxes. Two large, muscular men, their chests shining, naked, in the rain. One of them was old, Martin guessed over fifty, with a big stomach bulging over the belt of his baggy trousers and a shock of startling white hair that went oddly with a black straggly beard. Earlier that week, on other spying trips, Martin had decided he must be the grandfather. Although how many granddads were as fit and strong as this one was?

The other man – the son? – was in his early thirties, maybe. He was lean, but powerfully built, with no beer belly and no hair on his chest like the older man. His head was also almost hairless, shaven and gleaming black. As he worked, teeth glistened whitely in a face that was very ugly,

rather frightening.

The men were swinging huge sledgehammers, one after the other, from opposite sides of the long square stake they were driving into the ground beside the gates. As each blow landed, Martin saw the man who had made it rise slightly on the box beneath him, then settle as he swung back for the next one. As that hammer whirled away behind, the opposite one crashed down onto the stake. It was like a great machine.

Nearby stood a boy of sixteen or so – the "grandson", in Martin's mind. He was tall and thin and not powerful at all.

Nor was he stripped to the waist, but wore jeans and a coloured shirt, and a woolly hat on his head, pulled low at the back and ears. At his feet, under a coat, Martin could make out the edge of his ghetto-blaster, which was flooding the air with music. Martin realised, with a little jolt, that the big men were striking their alternate blows in time with it.

Beside the boy, leaning against the fence, was the reason for the work. A large square board, glistening with rain and paint, that was to be bolted to the upright when it had been driven deep enough. It would face the road, beside the gate, and be visible to passers-by and drivers.

It read, in big black letters on the white: Starkey, Raven and Son – Builders Suppliers.

Underneath, in red, it added: "We Mean Business".

Watching as the mighty, rhythmic blows fell in time to the driving music, Martin could well believe it.

# CHAPTER SIX

Despite the way his mates went on, Martin's first bad moment over the new neighbours came with his mum. He kicked himself, because it happened through carelessness – he forgot to tread quite warily enough. The problem was, in reality, that he did not know exactly why he needed to be careful with his parents, he just knew he did. They had a view of things that he did not fully understand, and somehow on this subject they were watching him.

It had been more than a week now, since they had moved in, and the first weekend had passed off without incident. Bolly, Cy and Snatch had come over on the Saturday as usual, but the spying plans they had talked about at school had come to nothing. The two big men, the thin youth and his ghetto-blaster, the woman and her little baby, had left at shortly after nine o'clock that morning, dressed up to the nines and in their car, a battered Volvo. The kids had ventured their heads above the wall, and been amazed by the way the yard had changed. But they had not dared go in.

"It's fantastic," said Bolly. "It's not like the same place. Old Man Quigley wouldn't recognise it."

"Yeah," said Martin. "They've done eleven skips at least, eleven that I counted, anyway. Quigley's junk just didn't touch the sides. They chucked the lot."

In a curious way, he felt a touch of pride, as if he'd had a part in all the work. At least, he'd watched a lot of it . . .

"They're big," he added, almost confused by his reaction. "I saw them shifting RSJs one afternoon. The two of them, the old ones. They took one end each and swung them till they'd got them really going. Then the beardie one gives it 'Waahay!' and it flies through the air and crashes in the lorry. They moved six of them. Amazing."

"Waahay!" repeated Cy. "Hey, minta!"

"What's an RSJ?" asked Bolly, less impressed.

And Snatch, showing off, said: "Reinforced steel joist. *Six* of them? Hell, Martin, they must be strong!"

"Yeah," he agreed. "They're strong. If one of them got hold of you, it wouldn't be like Old Man Quigley and his stick, it would be curtains. They'd break your back as soon as look at you. They're frightening."

It was a dry day at last, quite sunny, and they obviously couldn't waste it just staring over people's walls. But the yard, neatly laid out with stacks of bricks and scaffolding, piles of different coloured sands and baulks of timber, was very tempting, like a promised land.

"I suppose they've got a guard dog, too?" said Snatch. His voice was almost wistful. "A Rottweiler, is it? Or a Dobermann? No one bothers with boring old Alsatians any more."

"They don't need a dog," said Martin. "Why would you need a dog if you were like a tank yourself? They could tear a guard dog's head off with their bare hands. I'm telling you."

"Yah, bet me!" went Snatch. "That's crazy that is, Martin. No man could beat a Rottweiler. They're invincible."

The argument was stupid, but it passed the time. They slid down from the wall and along the alleyway, and ended up in the road. There was a small fair setting up in the meadows by the river, according to Cy's information, so they thought they'd walk along and see. Passing the front of the yard, Martin pointed out the sign to them.

"See that stake?" he said. "They drove that in just like a tent-peg. Two big hammers, bang-bang, bang-bang. I watched them. Terrifying."

Bolly read aloud: "Starkey, Raven and Son – Builders Suppliers. We Mean Business."

"It ought to say 'Trespassers will be ate'," said Cy, and was pleased to get a good laugh for it. He tried to carry the joke along. "Hey, that's why they don't want a dog, Martin! They'd have to fight it for the food! You know, the trespassers. The bones. Oh, never mind."

"Don't call us," said Bolly, "we'll call you. Come on, let's suss out this funfair. Who's got any dosh? We need some for the church fête tomorrow, remember. Mum'll kill us if we can't buy off her stall."

"So whose hard luck is that?" said Martin, who unlike the other three was not made to go to church. "I've got eighty pee, I'll be all right!"

"Tight git," said Snatch. "I've got eleven! I'll arm wrestle you for some! I'll take the lot off you!"

The builders yard was soon forgotten. There were – sometimes – better things to do.

It was in the middle of the following week, in fact, that Martin got into trouble, and at first it was only very minor. He had started on his homework late, for once, because as he had come in through the back gate at tea-time, he had heard barking from the end of the alleyway. It was faint, but deep and hollow. A big dog, somewhere – very big.

For a moment he had struggled with his conscience, but he had lost. He pulled the bag off his shoulder, dropped it in his garden, and scooted out into the alleyway again. His mouth was rather dry as he began to climb the wall, and his palms were damp. He had visions of a Rottweiler, at least. Two, maybe. Big and dangerous.

To his surprise, there was nothing to be seen. The lorry was not in its usual place, nor was the Volvo. The back door stood open, so someone must be in, but no work was going on. He neither heard nor saw any other sign of dogs, not the faintest echo of another bark. Coincidence, he guessed, big dogs somewhere else.

At home, though, his concentration on his schoolwork was not good. He kept thinking of the black men, and

*Bogeymen*

imagining a guard dog hidden away somewhere, perhaps. He had a clear picture in his mind of him climbing the wall, and the monstrous hound leaping for his throat. He could laugh it off, convince himself that he was barmy, but he could not get his mind locked on to work. He was at the kitchen table as always, but time ran away with him. His mother, preparing food, kept quiet as long as she could, but at ten to six she spoke.

"Martin, love, you'll have to clear those books away. Dad'll be home in a minute. Go upstairs."

"Aw, Mum. You know I can't work on that table. I've nearly finished."

His mother had a bunch of knives and forks in her hand.

"You're running late. Is it hard, or something? What particular branch of the tree of knowledge are you plucking the fruit from tonight?"

Martin grinned at her.

"No need to be sarcastic. Geography. I can't concentrate, that's all."

She plonked the cutlery down, smiling broadly.

"You never could in that subject, could you? You don't even know where the village shops are! Idle little devil."

"Mum," said Martin, without thinking. "Where do that lot come from?"

Her face was blank.

"What lot?"

"You know. That lot at the end. Stark Raving and Bonkers."

He should have been warned by her face, which stiffened slightly. But he did not notice.

"How should I know, love? They've only been here a couple of weeks. I haven't spoken to them yet."

Martin looked up from his diagram of continental drift. He was slightly startled by this idea.

"Spoken?" he said. "Are you going to speak to them?"

The warning signs were clearer. He could read concern and puzzlement quite plainly in his mother's face. It was a look that was inviting him to dig a grave and put his foot in it.

She said briskly: "Of course I'm going to speak to them. They're new neighbours. I don't want to bother them before they settle down, that's all."

"Oh," he said. He found he could not stop himself. "But where do you *think* they'll be from, anyway? Jamaica?"

"Jamaica!" She raised her eyebrows comically, to make a joke of it. "Well, more like London, I should think. Or Liverpool, or Birmingham, or Manchester. Anywhere, I don't know!"

"No," said Martin, doggedly. "I mean really. What's their real country."

It was a balance point. She could go either way. Her eyes were narrowed, and she did not speak for several seconds. Suddenly, she swung a chair round and sat opposite him, at the table.

"Martin," she said. "What are you trying to say to me? They could come from England really, you do know that, don't you? Just because we don't have many black people round here doesn't mean it isn't normal. They're people, just like you and me. Just what is the problem?"

To Martin's great relief, he heard the front door opening. His dad was home from work.

"In the kitchen, Jim," called Mum. Her voice was bright and normal. To Martin she said: "Get those books off, quickly. Get them upstairs. Dad will be tired, don't give him any nonsense, please."

"Hallo," said Dad, appearing in the doorway. "Hallo, Sunshine. Good day at school? What nonsense would that be, when it's out?"

Martin was silent. When his father came home tired he could be difficult. He bundled up the books.

"Secret is it?" said Dad, cheerfully. "Come on, you know I'm nosey. What's going on?"

He clearly wasn't tired. His broad, open face was positively sunny. Mum, knowing him inside out, relented.

"Oh, it's just Martin being silly," she said. "He's been

telling me about the neighbours. He thinks they come from Outer Space."

"Mum!"

Mr Turner ruffled his son's hair.

"Both feet firmly on the ground, from what I've heard," he said. "The middle one's been down the club already, looking for a place. Head like a bullet and goes like a bullet, apparently. Bowls like a man machinegun."

"Oh," said Mum. "Cricket."

"Well, it figures, doesn't it?" asked Dad. "The old racial stereotypes and so on. What do you say, Sunshine?"

But Martin did not understand and he did not pretend to. He took his books upstairs, glad that a real row had been avoided. He was interested in the cricketing, however. He thought the others would be, too. That was what black men were meant to be like, wasn't it? "Head like a bullet and goes like a bullet. A man machinegun."

So they were dangerous, and they were hard. Even his father admitted it. They were not men to be messed with.

He went down to his tea hoping that the subject would not be raised again.

# CHAPTER SEVEN

For a couple more weekends, the good times lasted. Snatch wanted to do something positive about the black men, but not even he could come up with a suggestion. Bolly agreed with him that they should take some sort of action, although she had no idea what, while Cy was merely terrified. He thought the fearsome neighbours should be left alone to live their strange and dangerous lives, and Martin, challenged to agree or disagree, did both or neither rather cleverly. He had a hollow feeling, though, that it could not last.

It was the dog aspect that got to Snatch the strongest.

"They've got to get one," he said, one pleasant afternoon. They were in the attic hideout, and Cy was perched up in the dormer. They'd taken turns to peer out at the builders yard, where work was going on and reggae was being played. "It stands to reason, someone's going to rob them one day if they don't get a dog. They've got to get one."

"You sound as if you want them to," said Bolly. "Have you got a death wish, Pearson? Does the idea of being crunched up like butchers' bones turn you on?"

It was too warm to fight, so Snatch just flicked a piece of dirt at her. He was sprawling on the mattress.

"What I mean," he said, "in words of one syllable for a half-wit, is that we've got to act before they do. I do *not* want to be bitten on the bum by a Dobermann, thanks very much. Which means we should do something fast."

"Yeah, yeah," Bolly replied dismissively. "So you've said before. I'll tell you what, when are you going to do something more than talk? You're just a bigmouth, you are. Where's the action?"

This was fighting talk. Cy, whose head had been half-in, half-out of the window, lowered himself towards the chair-back, blinking from the sun outside.

"Crikey," he said, quietly. "Steady on, Boll."

Martin could see that Snatch was working himself up, despite the lazy heat. He decided to take a hand in saving Bolly's neck.

"Ah," he said, "but what you don't know, any of you, is that we're too late already. They've—"

"What!" exploded Snatch. He rolled over on the mattress and pulled himself upright. Bolly was reprieved. "They've got one? What is it?"

On the spot, Martin blushed slightly.

"I haven't seen it yet," he said, "but it's definitely coming. They've been building it a kennel."

Snatch was excited. Cy was wobbling on the chair-back. Bolly had stood, and was wiping sweat from underneath her fringe.

"What sort of kennel? Can we see it from the window? Hell, Martin, when was this?"

"I saw it a couple of days ago. Thursday, I think, after school. It's not just any kennel, neither. It's made of bricks and stuff, not wood."

"Wow!" went Cy. "It'll be a Rottweiler for certain. Lots, maybe!"

Maybe, thought Martin, it's not a kennel at all, it's hell's big for a kennel. Too late to back down now, though.

Snatch's thin face, underneath the shock of black hair, had come alive.

"Has it got the roof on yet?" he said. "How quickly can they finish it? It's Saturday today, you can't build a brick kennel in two days, can you? It'd be too wet to put a dog in, anyway, it needs time to dry out. I've helped my dad with brick."

Martin's good feeling dropped away. He could almost guess what Snatch was going to say next.

But Bolly said it for him.

"We'll have to really go," she said. "Before it's ready for the dogs. We'll have to get in quick."

Martin said: "It's got no roof yet. It may not be a kennel, even. I don't know. It may ... I mean ..."

Snatch and Bolly were disbelieving. Was he trying to get out of it? He smiled, sickly.

"That's no reason not to go in, though, is it?" he said. "It would give us more times, that's all. More opportunities."

Cy's voice was squeaky.

"But I don't want to," he said. "What about the chickens' blood? What about the goats?"

"It'll be dangerous," said Bolly, ignoring her brother. "I mean, Old Man Quigley used to chase us, but he never really minded, did he? This lot'd break our legs."

"Are you game?" Snatch asked Martin, bluntly. His voice and face were hard, he was suspicious.

"But what about the woman?" wailed Cy. "What if she hexes us? What about her spells?"

"Of course I'm game," said Martin. He was aware of how red he was. What *would* these people do? Maybe the goats and chicken blood were not so crazy, after all. "Of course I'm coming in," he went on. "The trouble is . . . well, you know . . . we've got to find a time. A time when they're not there."

"Ah well," said Snatch, "that's your job, isn't it? You live next door, nearly. That's for you to judge."

"Help me down!" screeched Cy. "I'm slipping!"

Bolly jumped, but she was too late. Cy's short legs pushed the chair over as he tried to balance on it. He tried to grab his sister, missed, and crashed onto the mattress. A burst of dust flew upwards. Cy lay crying, dirt mixed with his tears.

"They've put a hex on him already," Snatch said.

Only Bolly laughed.

# CHAPTER EIGHT

Oddly, it was another "bad moment" over the neighbours –
in fact, a rather violent row with his father – that finally
gave Martin the courage to do the deed. He had got
involved in talking to his mother after a late tea, and his
father had walked in on it. This time he had not come home
from work in a good mood, he was grey with tiredness. His
tea was ruined in the oven, he had been forced to do three
hours overtime, and Mrs Turner was too sick of Martin's
silliness to cover up for him.

It had started because he had been worrying about
Snatch and Bolly and the raid. He had had two sleepless
nights worrying about it, and even Cy's ridiculous nonsense
had begun to seem half real. If they went in, he felt, they
would be caught, and something terrible would happen. He

had been trying to find out from his mother what it might be, at the worst.

At first, Mrs Turner had been sympathetic. She had noted from his pale face that he had lost sleep, and wanted to find out why. But Martin, naturally, had not been able to tell the truth, so had wrapped it up in ramblings and evasions. She had worked out that it was something to do with the neighbours, but had no idea what.

Had he spoken to them? No. Had they shown any sign of knowing he existed? No. Had they upset him in some way, without even having any contact? No. What then? Martin, caught with no cover story, mumbled something about voodoo, and zombies, and the walking dead. By the time his dad came in the situation was bad, and within minutes he and Martin were shouting at each other.

"But who told you? It's absolute raving nonsense, Martin! Where did you *get* this from?"

Mum, by now, was trying to calm things down. It was getting ugly.

"Oh come on, love," she told her husband. "It's only a daft kids' tale."

"It's not daft! It's vile! It's racist nonsense!"

"But they *aren't* like us!" shouted Martin. "They act completely different! All that reggae all the time! I can't sleep!"

"But that's just the son," said Mum. "He's only sixteen, Martin. When we mentioned it, they turned it down. You haven't heard it recently, have you? At night?"

That was true, but Martin was not forced to say so, luckily. His father's face was wild.

"Never mind the reggae! What about the chickens' blood? What about the goats?"

It had been Martin's stupidest mistake, to mention them. But he would not climb down.

"It's their religion! It's what they do! Bolly says—"

His father interrupted.

"Martin, just shut up, will you? Before I really lose my temper. I hear enough of this tommyrot down at the factory, it drives me up the wall. I won't have any son of mine coming out with it, OK?"

He had brought his voice down a pitch or two. He was trying consciously to regain control. Martin assessed the situation, and decided to go on arguing.

"But it's—" he started. His father's eyes went wide with rage.

"But nothing! Go to bed! Now!"

His shout had almost taken out the kitchen window. Martin gulped. He dared not speak. His mother shrugged. She was pale.

"You'd better go," she said. "It's late in any case."

It wasn't late, it wasn't half-past nine.

"But it's not fair," he began. Then stopped. He glanced at his father, then away. He went to bed.

By the time the subject of the raid came up again, Martin had sorted himself out. He was still afraid about the black men, but his fear was mixed with anger and resentment. He resented them for being there, he resented his father for not understanding what it meant, he resented himself for thinking they were dangerous, or that different from anybody else – although, deep down, he still believed it, which also filled him with resentment. Overall, he wanted to *show* somebody, and out of that desire slowly formed a plan.

Cricket was the key, but Martin thought it through very carefully before he said anything to his friends. In fact, on the day he sprung his trap, cricket would have been impossible, it was lashing down with rain. In the morning all four of them had done things with their parents, as it was Saturday, not meeting in the hideout until after lunch. They were damp but warm, so they messed about quite happily. They had some drink and their weekly sweets. They played violent games mixed up with long relaxes. During one of these, the builders yard came up.

"There's nothing for it," Snatch said, from the mattress. "We've got to go in there. We're dribbling our lives away. We've got to move."

Cy, like a laboratory rat responding to a food bell, gaped with fear.

"What, today? We can't!"

His sister raised her eyes to heaven.

"Stupid! Not today. We'd get soaked, wouldn't we? Soakeder."

"But we can't go *any* day," whined Cy. "I thought we'd sorted that. There's a dog now, isn't there?"

"No, there's not a dog," said Snatch. "There may not even be a kennel, Martin says he isn't sure. Martin said he'd find out things, didn't he? Like the best time, for instance. That's what we sorted out."

"Didn't we, Martin?" Bolly added. Her voice, too, dripped with sarcasm. "Have you done it yet?"

"Or are you like Cy?" said Snatch. "Chicken! Chick-chick, chick-chick chicken? Cluuuck cluck-cluck-cluck-cluck-cluck!"

He jumped to his feet and flapped his elbows in and outwards from his body, with Bolly laughing.

"It's not a case of being chicken," Cy said, hunching deeper in his damp anorak. "It's a case of being mad or sane. They aren't just black, those blokes, they're giants. And there's the spells."

Snatch hooted.

"If they turned you into a frog it would be a positive

improvement," he said. "You'd be quite good looking as a frog."

Martin, who was silently whittling at a piece of wood, smiled to himself. It occurred to him that Snatch and Bolly felt very safe, and very smug. They thought they'd never have to put their bravery to the test. He kept his head low.

"Yeah, jolly funny," Cy said. "But—"

"But nothing," interrupted Snatch. "We organised to go in when the time was ripe, and if we don't go in they've beat us, haven't they? What's your excuse, Martin? Chick-chick-chicken just like Cy? Scared of the nasty witch?"

He was in front of Martin, and Bolly moved to his side. Martin whittled for a few seconds more, then raised his eyes. Their faces were flushed, excited at the attack. He stayed very calm.

"I've been thinking, actually," he said. "We couldn't do it on a weekday."

Snatch, despite himself, showed interest. He knew that Martin was driving at something.

"But?" he said. "Go on."

"But there's a one-day match next Saturday," said Martin. "They're cricket crazy, all of them."

"Hah-*hey*!" said Snatch, getting the drift immediately. "I *like* it!"

Bolly, quite definitely, was not half so keen.

"Hold on," she said. "What's that got to do with it? What are you saying, Martin?"

"Oh come on, Bolly," said Martin. He was right, and it elated him. When it came down to it, Bolly was afraid. "They'll be at the match, won't they? All of them. Stark, Raving, Bonkers *and* the woman."

"But she's got a little baby."

"They're cricketing mad. The baby, too, I shouldn't wonder. My father said they haven't missed a match."

"So we can do a raid!" said Snatch. "Martin, that's terrific!"

Right about Bolly, wrong about Snatch. Snatch was not afraid at all, Snatch had not been bluffing him. Oh hell, thought Martin. He said, carefully: "Mark you, it'd still be risky. I mean—"

Cy said: "It'd be broad daylight! We might get caught!"

"Well done!" crowed Snatch. "Mastermind lives!"

Martin's mouth had dried a little.

Oh hell, he thought.

# CHAPTER NINE

Like a good general, Snatch did not try to hide the hard-
ships and the dangers from his soldiers. Nor did he lurk
behind the battle lines in safety while they took all the risks.
The following Saturday, he hid with the others by the gates
and watched until the Volvo had driven away, and he led
them back round the terrace and down the alleyway to the
high wall. There, he dealt with early signs of mutiny.

"I don't want to go," said Cy. "I could've gone to Auntie
Mary's with my mum. I wish I'd gone to Auntie Mary's."

Bolly – as nervous as a kitten – would probably have
snapped at him, but Snatch stepped in.

"Look, Cy," he said, "don't worry, eh? We saw them go,
and they won't come back, will they? We saw them pack
their cricket bags in the car, and the weather's terrific. We

haven't got a thing to worry about."

"Yeah," said Cy. "But I'm—"

"Shut up!" his sister said – and Snatch shushed her.

"No," he said. "Cy's got a right to be nervy. I'm nervy, too, Cy, I'm terrified. But we've got to do it, right? I'll go first and do a recce, then you come, Bolly. Then Cy, then Martin, OK?"

Martin was impressed. He was frightened, but he didn't reckon he'd have admitted it. What's more, he didn't even believe Snatch was, whatever he said. He shared a smile with Bolly, and saw she felt the same. Snatch didn't give them much chance to complain, did he? Even Cy managed a little smile.

"What's a recce? I've never heard of that. Is it like a wreck?"

Snatch shook his head. He had his hands on the loose bricks, ready to climb.

"It's short for reconnaissance. Having a dekko, a good old shufti. Hang on, watch nothing falls on you."

In three seconds he was at the top. He looked into the yard, then swung his legs over.

"Clear," he said. "Come on, Boll. You're not afraid, are you?"

In half a minute, Martin and Cy were alone on the safe side. Cy, his terror coming back, grabbed Martin's sleeve.

"I wish we hadn't done it, Martin. I've got a tummy-ache. I'm scared she'll hex me, honest, I need the lav. You'll let me go home, won't you?"

Martin knew that Snatch had planned this out. He'd be behind the wall enjoying it. Forcing the pair of them to be brave.

"Look," he said, half-angrily. "We've got to do it, we're all mates. And anyway, it's tommyrot, all that spell stuff. Killing goats, and so on. It's stupid garbage."

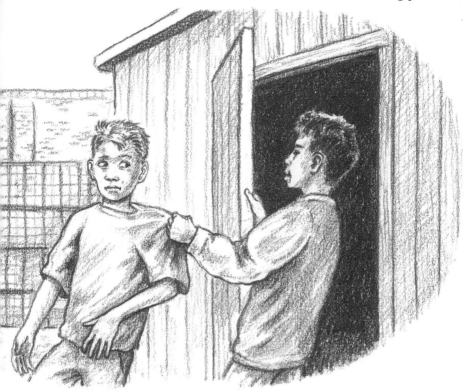

"But my dad..." began Cy. His sister's head appeared above the wall.

"Come on! For the honour of the Fisher family! Gawd help us..."

And Martin pushed him forward to the wall.

Inside the yard, all four of them felt very strange. It was the first time since the new people had moved in. It was definitely spooky.

"God," said Bolly, her voice breathy. "It's all so different, isn't it? It's not like looking over the wall, neither. It's such good stuff."

Martin nodded. His stomach had gone hollower and hollower. This was serious.

"I told you, didn't I? Skiploads, they shifted. They just chucked Old Man Quigley's stock out. All of it. Straight down the tip."

Snatch said: "You wouldn't chuck this stuff, would you? This is real."

He picked up a new brick from a neat stack. He weighed it in his hand, as if to throw. Cy panicked.

"Don't chuck it, Snatch! What if they come back? It's worth money, this. Thousands!"

Snatch gave him a grin. He put the brick back. He did not even drop it.

"Shut it," he said. He moved to a shed door, and began to open it. "We've got all afternoon, they won't come back. Martin. Come and look in here with me. You two, round the back."

"I'm not messing about with anything, though," said Bolly. "Not like Quigley's stuff."

Snatch pulled Martin to the open door.

"Quit whining, can't you?" he told Bolly. "Just go and have a look around."

After the brightness, the shed was black and worrying.

There were only two small windows, high and dirty, and the door had swung shut behind them. The boys stood still for a few moments, waiting to get used to it. It smelt strongly, of pleasant things, like creosote and shavings and new sacks.

"Not like the old days," said Martin. "D'you remember that stink there used to be? Horrible."

"Dirty old git, old Quigley was," said Snatch. "It's funny though, them being clean. Not what you'd expect, is it? You know."

Martin did not reply. He thought of his father. Of the "tommyrot he heard at work". He moved forward, touched a brand new rack of tools.

"What'd they say if they found out we'd been in?" he said. "Now it's proper stuff? Mine half killed me last time Old Man Quigley moaned."

Snatch nodded in the gloom.

"Yeah. Mine made me promise. Never, ever again." He paused. "It's only a laugh though, isn't it? I mean."

"They don't understand," said Martin. "That's the trouble. But if this lot caught us..."

"They won't. Don't think about it. I mean, in a way, it's safer, isn't it?"

"How do you mean?"

"Well," replied Snatch. "If we pick our time right. Like

today. No one around to catch us. No one to tell our dads."

He had moved forward to the bench. Underneath it was a pile of boxes, with tangled wire and pieces of metal piled around them. He was pulling at something caught up among the clutter.

Martin said unhappily: "Well, we couldn't count on it, could we? Today we're lucky, but . . . you know."

"Yeah. But Old Man Quigley was always on the premises, wasn't he? We never had a clear run. Look, a weighing thing. Brass."

With a jerk, he freed the object and held it up. It was old, and big, a brass spring balance with metal hooks at either end. It was the length of Martin's arm. Martin did not want to touch, he wanted to have nothing to do with it.

"Just a bit of junk," he said. "Put it back, Snatch."

"What I mean," said Snatch, rubbing at the brass with the ball of his hand to polish it, "is we could come in again. Next time there's a cricket match, say. Until they get a dog, if you didn't just make that up. We could come in regular."

Martin's discomfort grew. Then it sharpened to fear as he heard a shout. It was Cy, and his voice was tight with alarm.

"Bolly! Here! Help!"

They heard Bolly hiss to shut him up. If they could hear inside the shed . . . Oh God, thought Martin. Without a word, he and Snatch rushed for the door.

Outside, they followed the noise to locate the others. The noise of Cy wailing and Bolly shushing him. They ran round behind another shed, past stacks of fresh-cut wood and scaffolding. They saw Bolly and her brother beside the new shed, the kennel Martin had tried to scare them with. Surely there was not a dog, after all?

"What's up?" said Snatch, urgent and low. Then: "Oh my God."

"See," said Cy. He was shaken but defiant, proved right at last. "See, it's all *true*!"

Inside the small brick hut, lying on its stomach and eyeing them glassily, was an enormous goat.

"See," said Cy, for the third time. "I told you, didn't I? They kill them. They drink their blood. A *sacrifice*."

"I think we ought to go," said Bolly.

# CHAPTER TEN

In bed that night, for the first time in his life, Martin got himself into a state he felt he could not handle. His mind was crowded with a million thoughts that boiled down to one: he was involved in something criminal, and he would be found out. Then what would happen?

At first, trying to put it into words that he could understand, could deal with, he told himself it was his conscience that was troubled. He had helped steal from the builder's yard, and he knew that it was wrong. But as the evening ground slowly onwards, he admitted to himself that it was largely fear. Whatever Snatch and Bolly said, they would be found out and they would suffer. They were no longer dealing with a bad-tempered old eccentric with a stick, they were dealing with a real business, with people who knew their stock, who had paid good money for it, who would find out it was gone. Who would be furious.

The night was warm, and through his open window Martin heard the faint strains of reggae on the breeze. It was not loud, and that realisation added shame to the worries tumbling through his mind. Unlike Cy, he did not believe that the neighbours would do dreadful things to him when they found out, that was absurd. It was not black magic that frightened him, not spells and voodoo, but the police. Then he saw the goat in his mind's eye, much bigger than he thought goats ought to be, brown-coated, with enormous glossy eyes like gobstoppers, and the confusion flooded back. They had a goat, there was no denying it. So *why?*

After shame, after confusion, there was anger. One could always fall back on anger when all else failed. Martin rolled savagely over, balled up on the bed, burying himself deeper in the tangle of his duvet. It was Snatch's fault, it was all his fault and he'd done it quite deliberately. If Snatch had only listened, not been such a selfish jerk, it would not have happened. Snatch and Bolly, Bolly egging him on, grinning her gappy-tooth grin, not caring because she lived two miles away. Like all of them, safe across the river and the fields, safe on the other side of town, safe as flaming houses.

"Ooh," groaned Martin. "Ooohoohoh." He listened to

himself, interested. Groaning out loud even seemed to help, momentarily. "Ooooohoohohoooh." That was it, maybe. Blame it all on Snatch and Bolly.

"Just lift it up," Snatch had told him. "Just lift it up and stop arguing. You're yellow."

His voice was testy, he was as afraid as any of them, there was no doubt of that. But Snatch was out to prove something.

"Look," said Martin. "We've done what we said we would, we've come into the yard. Why nick anything?"

Cy, standing at the bottom of the wall, had been white with fear. He'd been practically on the verge of wetting himself, his legs were crossed.

"It's all new stuff," he was whining. "We'll get into *awful* trouble."

Martin, astride the wall, reluctantly reached downwards. Snatch and Bolly were shoving a long roll of chicken wire up at him, a roll as thick as a man. Beside them, in the yard still, was another one. Propped against it was the brass spring balance.

"Cy's right," he said. "For once he is dead right. They might even call the law."

"Ah dry up, chicken," said Snatch. "Martin Turner, you're so chicken."

"That's why we've got chicken wire," said Bolly.

"Especially for you."

But her face was pale and anxious.

"Hurry up," she added. "For God's sake, Martin – pull!"

In the hideout, after a tense and silent scurry along the alleyway, the divisions in the camp continued. Bolly and Snatch set out to hide the rolls of wire underneath some rotten carpet, while Cy and Martin did the worrying. Cy was crying quietly, because he'd wet down his leg trying to have a pee in the back garden and Bolly had smacked his head. He'd tried to run home, but she'd tripped him up and smacked him harder. Martin was throwing sullen questions, goading Snatch, who refused to lose his temper.

"It would have been rubbish otherwise, that's why," he said patiently. He was talking to Martin as to a sulky five-year-old. "We went in there to show old Stark and Bonkers we weren't scared. It would have been rubbish to come out empty-handed."

"That's lies," said Martin, hotly. "We didn't go to show them anything, we went for us, for fun! Not to steal! Not to get in trouble! We went for *us*!"

Bolly did not like them arguing. She was conciliatory.

"It's only a bit of wire, though," she said. "There were lots and lots of rolls. They'll never miss a couple, will they?"

Martin savagely kicked the spring balance. It bounced across the floor to Snatch's feet.

"What about this, then?" he said. "It's solid brass."

Snatch bent and picked it up. He held it horizontally and tried to pull it open like a chest-expander. He failed.

"It's not worth a fortune, it's knackered. We didn't nick anything good. Nothing you'd go to prison for."

Cy, sniffling in a corner, reacted as if he'd been prodded with a pin. His eyes went wide.

"*Prison!*"

Bolly got instantly ratty.

"Oh don't be such a moron, Cy," she snapped. "Kids don't go to prison. Don't show me up all the time!"

Snatch leered.

"Reform school," he told Cy. "Youth custody. Borstal. You live on porridge and get caned ten times a day. God, you're stupid."

Fed up with the game, he walked decisively to the fireplace. It was tiled, full of old blackened rubbish. In winter, they sometimes risked a fire there, burning magazines and papers. Snatch bent and stuffed the spring balance as far up as he could, well out of sight. Soot spattered down as he jammed it so that it would not fall. He straightened up, brushing at his hands.

"Satisfied? No one'll ever find it there, will they? You're

chicken, the pair of you. Chicky-chick-chick-chicken. You're pathetic."

There was an awkward silence. Bolly wanted to make a new mood. She sympathised with Martin, in a way.

"I know!" she said. "I'll ask Uncle Les! He gave us two litres of coke once, didn't he, for some of Quigley's stuff? He might want the wire for his garden."

"See?" said Snatch. "See, Martin? A couple of days, that's all. What could possibly go wrong in a couple of measly days?"

Martin, lying in his bed, had stopped his groaning. He was on his back, eyes open, staring sightlessly at the dark ceiling. He felt physically ill now, his breath kept quickening, he was almost panting, there was sweat on his forehead. He began to twist and turn once more, it was awful, it was torture, he could not make it stop, it was like creatures gnawing at his brain, like talons scratching at the inside of his skull. They would find out, they *must* find out, and something terrible would happen.

Downstairs, his mother's sewing machine whirred. It was Saturday night and his father had gone to the pub with friends. Martin groaned, not loudly any more, in a sort of agony.

It was not the kind of thing you could confess to, was it? That you'd been stealing things. That you'd gone back on a promise about the builders yard. What would she say? She'd be appalled, ashamed of him.

Martin rolled out of bed, and clutched his head between his hands.

He would have to talk to her, to tell her something.

He just could not stand this torment any more.

# CHAPTER ELEVEN

When the crunch came, Martin could not tell the truth. He went downstairs in the half-darkness, he dithered outside the kitchen door, in the end he gently turned the handle. But he knew before he entered that he could not tell the truth.

The weirdest thing, perhaps, was that his mother appeared to be expecting him. He held his breath as he eased the kitchen door open, but she knew immediately he was behind her. Nor was she surprised. Although it was almost eleven, she took it naturally, as if they'd agreed earlier that he should come and chat.

"Hallo, love," she said. "Can't you sleep? Is it the machine?"

He shook his head.

"No. Can't hear it except every now and then. What you making?"

She gave him a sideways look. Curtains for his gran, as he already knew. She did not comment, though.

"What's the trouble, then?" She laughed. "Not the reggae, is it? Not the naughty black men? What d'you call them, Starkers Raver and Bonking? Racist little devil!"

"Stark," he said. "Oh, Mum. Be serious. I'm worried."

"Worried? What about?"

The lies came easily. He hadn't thought about them. Not lies, exactly. Suppression of the truth.

"Oh, silly, stupid things. Police. Prisons. Oh, I don't know."

The radio was playing on the table. Soft, smoochy music. Late night romantic rubbish. But his mother's face was calm and intelligent, waiting for more.

Feeling helpless, Martin went and sat down on a chair. He did not face her, he took her sideways on. Mrs Turner did not complain, just let it ride. She waited.

"I know it's silly," he said, "but people talk. About it. Teachers go on and on. About if you do things. You know, crime. Against the law. Mr Barron says there's a crime wave on." His eyes brightened, he had remembered some useful details. "He says most crime's committed by young men. Almost boys. You know."

His mother was examining a line of stitching.

"Yes," she said. "That's true. I suppose most of us grow out of it. But why should you lose sleep over the crime wave?"

She pressed her foot pedal and the machine ate cloth. Martin watched her bent head. Brown, curly hair with a little white mixed in. He didn't want to hurt her, which made it so much harder.

"Oh, no reason." He tried to make his voice sound light and confident. "I just can't get it out of my head, that's all. I mean, if people do do crime so young . . . what happens to them?"

He remembered Cy's white face. His fear of prison, and Snatch's jeers. He licked his lips. The whirring stopped. Mum raised her face to him. He did not look away.

"Prison, you mean? What sort of punishment they get? If they're caught?"

Her eyes were keen and brown, assessing him. Martin nodded, dumbly. Again she waited.

"That sort of thing," he said, at last. "I mean, it's totally stupid, I haven't done anything myself. Well, obviously. It's just that . . . well . . . what if I had?"

"Martin. Darling. I'll have to ask you this straight out, love. You're not in any trouble, are you? Honestly?"

"No! I told you! Look, if you're not going to believe

me . . ."

He had faced her boldly for a moment, trying to achieve a flash of anger, which would have helped. But he felt hunted, not angry, and he feared his eyes would show it. He shrugged, a convulsion, to hide the fact that he had to look away.

"All right, I believe you. You're my son, I trust you, Martin. So tell me. Why do you want to know? Just . . . spit it out."

He was staring at the floor. There was a stain on the rug that was like a tortoise. He wished he had a shell. She trusted him. And he was telling lies. It was hard.

"It's nothing really, honestly," he said. It probably wasn't, he wasn't lying that much. "It's just . . . oh, there's some bad kids at school, that's all. We thought they might . . . well, go to Borstal or something. I mean, how old do you have to be?"

"Borstal? That's a blast from the past, they don't call it that these days, surely? Funny how these words stick around. But anyway, even in the old days when I was a girl . . . well, it depends, doesn't it? On what they've done, these kids. Stealing?"

"Yeah," he muttered. "I think so. Sort of. I mean – nothing valuable, I think it was an old spring balance or something. Just old junk."

Too specific. He shouldn't have said that. But she hadn't noticed, luckily.

"I don't think the value really matters, does it? Surely, if it belongs to someone and you take it, that's the—"

"Not *me*," he interrupted, quickly. "These kids!"

"Yes. I mean whoever takes it, naturally. It's stealing, isn't it?"

He was depressed. The tortoise was just a blob now. Soup, probably.

"Yeah, I suppose so. So what would happen to them? If they were caught? Would they go away? Get sent?"

The chair creaked as his mother rose. She came and stood beside him.

"Love, I honestly don't know. I could ask Dad, when he gets back from the pub. He might—"

She had tried to lay a hand on Martin's shoulder, but he pulled away.

"No!" It came out too sharply. He glanced at her, a swift smile to soften it. "No, I wouldn't bother, Mum. Telling Dad. It's not important. I was wondering, that's all. These kids..."

She straightened her back.

"People are very kind with kids," she said. "Lucky kids, whose mums and dads have jobs and houses and look respectable. That's what really matters in this world, that's what counts. You'd better get to bed now, love, it's late and you'll get cold in your pyjamas. You mustn't worry, though. About them. I expect they'll be all right, don't you?"

Martin nodded. He hoped so. Oh, he sincerely hoped so.

"You won't tell Dad, though, will you?" he said. "That I asked?"

"Why not?"

Their eyes held for a moment. He felt that she could see

inside his brain.

"He'll get the wrong idea. Please, Mum."

"He does get moods," she said. "But he's a terrific bloke, love. I won't do anything rash, OK?"

"Please, Mum. Don't tell him."

"Martin," she said. "I won't drop you in it. I promise. Now go to bed. He could be coming home. Go."

Until the moment he dropped off, Martin was quite certain he would not go to sleep that night. His last thought was about the stolen stuff. He would have to do something about it first thing in the morning. That was vital.

But what . . .?

# CHAPTER TWELVE

When he awoke, and for one minute afterwards, Martin was quite happy. The sun was shining through his thin curtains, and the air smelt sweet. He could hear some sheep bawling, not far distant, and a single, cracked church bell. Bolly and Cy would be going later, to Sunday school in the afternoon and to a service early in the evening. That alone made him feel good, because he did not have to bother. He had all day Sunday to . . . and it came back to him, with a lurch. He swung instantly out of bed and went to the bathroom. He would not waste a moment.

He got into the hideout a good half-hour before he was due to meet the others, which was a bad mistake. He uncovered the two rolls of wire, and he poked about up in the chimney till he felt the balance, although he did not pull it down. Until the others came, there was nothing he could do, except maybe worry. To make it worse, after ten minutes or so the reggae started up. Martin risked the chair-back and climbed into the dormer, craning his neck out to see the builders yard. The tall skinny youth was working there, in a garish tee shirt and his wild tea-cosy hat. Which neatly ruined one of Martin's half-thought-out plans – to simply chuck the gear back over the high wall and hope. When he heard footsteps on the twisted staircase, he was deep in gloom.

Snatch and Bolly, as expected, did not share his woes. In fact, it was almost as if they'd forgotten any danger. He launched straight into them, demanding that they do something, and they treated him like a fool.

"Do what?" said Bolly. "Get a magic wand and make it disappear? You're like my little brother, you are."

Cy had not come with her, and Martin had not asked why. He did not care.

"We've got to get it shifted," he said. "That's all. It's too near my house!"

"What, in broad daylight?" said Snatch. "With them working in the yard? You're crackers."

"We'd get seen," said Bolly. "You can't hide rolls of chicken wire up your jumper, Martin, can you?"

"You are as daft as Cy," said Snatch. "He wouldn't come

today at all. He's afraid the big black demons were going to get him. We're going to meet him by the river. Let's go now and mess about. It's boring here."

"No! We can't go . . . I mean . . ."

Bolly shook her head at him.

"You've got it bad, you have, Martin. There's nothing you can do, it's stupid worrying. Nothing's going to happen, is it? Not today. Nothing's changed since yesterday. We'll talk about it later. We'll sort it out."

Snatch was already by the door. He was impatient.

"Come on," he said. "I've got two quid. Don't be a drip, mate, don't be weedy. It's Sunday, Sunday funday!"

He turned, and began to clatter down the stairs. Like Bolly, he never seemed to fear they would collapse. Bolly touched Martin's arm, her face earnest.

"Look," she said, "I know you're worried, but I'll see Uncle Les tonight at church. I'll ask him, I bet he wants the stuff, you know Uncle Les. Forget it for a while."

It made sense, sort of. More sense than staying there, alone, and moping. Taking a kick at a roll of chicken wire, Martin followed her downstairs, determined to clear his mind and have some fun. He did it so successfully, in fact, that when his father raised the subject several hours later, at the end of lunch, it affected Martin like a bombshell. He had forgotten everything.

Being Sunday, it was a relaxed time, although his mum was slowly clearing things away. The teapot was on the table, and Martin was looking at a fairly new *Beano*, spread flat in front of him. His father's head was buried in a newspaper.

"Jim," said Mrs Turner, as she bustled past, "I'd appreciate it if you put that paper down, you know. You've hardly said a word through dinner."

Her tone was only mildly irritated. Sitting about and reading was a regular weekend routine. Dad lowered his paper to reply.

"Nothing much to say, was there? Anyway, it's rude to talk with your mouth full, eh Martin?"

Martin did not answer. His hand reached out to feel for his cup.

"Oh, there was one thing," said Dad, looking at Mrs Turner. "Did you hear about the raid? At Starkeys?"

Martin behaved like something from his comic. He jumped as if stung and slopped his tea everywhere.

"Steady on, old son!" said Dad. "I haven't read that bit yet!"

"Starkeys?" said Mum, her voice showing only minor interest. "What, our Starkeys?"

"Yes. I met one of them this morning, at the petrol station. The one with the shaved head. They're furious.

They're after someone's blood."

Martin stood. He felt sick. He did not know what to do or say.

"Mum. Have you got a cloth? I've spilt some tea."

She came to him smiling, a damp cloth in her hand. With the other one she patted his shoulder, pushed him back into his seat.

"Never mind," she said, "it'll mop up, love. What's been taken, Jim? Anything expensive? I'm not surprised they're angry."

"Angry's not in it. Hopping mad. Wild." He took the cloth to wipe a pool of tea his wife had missed. "I'm telling you, God help the thieves if they should ever catch them. They're terrors when they're roused, those West Indians. Martin? What's up with you?"

Martin's mouth was hanging slightly open. He still had his tea cup in his hand, three-quarters empty. He put it to his mouth and swigged noisily to hide the expression on his face.

"Manners of a pig, that boy," said Dad, indulgently. He gave the cloth back to Mrs Turner. "Yeah, they've found some of the stuff apparently, some chicken wire. It'd been chucked into the old corner shop, you know, Patterson's old place. They haven't finished checking yet, but they don't actually think there's a great deal been stolen, although you wouldn't believe it from the way they're going on. When they know exactly what they've lost they'll do a proper search of Patterson's tomorrow."

"Chicken wire's not much use," said Mum. "I mean, you'd not find fingerprints on that, would you? A detective wouldn't."

"That's right. The clincher, if they could find it, would be a big spring balance. They're pretty sure it's missing, although it might just be mislaid, and it's made of solid brass. Fingerprints galore. What's up, Martin?"

"Nothing. Can I get down, please? I just . . ."

He had got up from his chair. His mother was staring at him.

"A spring balance?" she said. "That's funny. You were talking about a spring balance, weren't you? Yesterday."

He tried to get a grip. He faced them.

"Er. Yeah. Yes. Some . . . some boys I know. Some of the kids. They said they'd found one. Over by the . . . the old dyeworks."

"*Found* one?" said Dad.

"Yeah. But I thought . . . I reckoned they might have nicked it. I thought they might . . . sort of . . . go to Borstal. That's why I asked you, Mum."

There was a bark of laughter from his father.

"Borstal! They wouldn't get the chance! They'll tear

them limb from limb, those black guys." Then he changed his tack, his eyes narrowed, his head moved forward to Martin's. "What exactly do you mean, though? By 'boys you know'? Are you quite certain you're not involved yourself? Are you quite sure you haven't done another Quigley?"

"No, Dad. Not me, honestly. Kids."

Dad stared at him, and Martin licked his lips, trying to do it secretly. Then, unexpectedly, his father relaxed. Apparently he believed him. He flopped back in his chair.

"Well, if they're mates of yours, Sunshine," he said, "I'd give 'em a warning, double quick. Get that balance back where they took it from, pronto. And wipe the fingerprints off first. If they want their skins to wear."

"Wouldn't it be more sense just to throw it away, Jim?" asked Mrs Turner.

"Rubbish. They're like bulldogs, these men. They'd never rest until they'd found the culprit. But if the balance turned up again ... well, they wouldn't be sure, would they? That it had ever gone in the first place. You tell them, Martin."

Martin was moving towards the door. He could not stay, the thoughts were churning in his head.

"They're not exactly mates," he said. His voice sounded terribly feeble to him. He tried to strengthen it. "Just kids.

Let them stew, for all I care."

He got through the door and began to climb the stairs. It was as if a great weight was on his shoulders. Dad, still in the kitchen, raised his voice.

"Well, tonight's the night, Sunshine." He was extremely jolly. "They're going to a free-and-easy at the cricket club, the lot of them. They're members now, you know."

Martin knew, of course he knew. But what hope could that give him? Could he work miracles? Was he meant to hop in there on his own? His mum and dad were home, in any case, with Dad probably watching him, just in case. They weren't stupid, either of them, unfortunately.

He surveyed his bedroom, patterned with warm sun. It felt like a prison.

# CHAPTER THIRTEEN

It was dark when Martin got to the hideout, but it was not dark enough. He had crept along the alleyway trembling with tension in case someone had turned into it and seen him – a boy in jeans and dark jumper with a pair of gloves on, on a summer evening. It seemed to him as if everything about him – even the way he walked – would have given him away. He was a burglar, a thief.

At the gap, though, he cursed the gloom. As he eased himself through, a glove jagged and tore. Imagining a noise behind him, Martin panicked and pulled harder. With a clang, a rusty piece of corrugated iron fell to the ground. It was a full minute before he could control his panting.

Not a burglar, he told himself as he crept cautiously across the jungly garden, not a thief. For one thing, he was doing it in reverse, he was going to do a break-in to return something. And for another – he stumbled heavily, making more noise – he did not have a torch, he was a total stumblebum. Get a grip, boy, get a grip, he told himself. If someone finds you now, you're up the creek without a paddle. Get a grip.

The stairs were the worst part. Inside the derelict shop it was pitchy, and the shaking, creaky timbers appeared to be ready to collapse at last. He had visions of them falling down on top of him, and him lying there in a pool of blood, undiscovered. Worse, bleeding. He saw a throbbing vein, the dark blood pumping out – and was surprised to discover that he was already at the top. A little light spilled through the skylight, making him feel better. He'd get the balance by that light, and make it down the stairs again. Then, safe outside, he'd wait until full dark before he climbed the wall. He had been given his chance to put things right, his fantastic stroke of luck, and he must not mess it up.

He had been on his bed when the chance had come, lying miserable and hopeless. Although it was early and he was fully dressed, he had not turned on his light, and would probably have pulled a cover across himself later and stayed put all night. Earlier he had sneaked downstairs and listened to his parents talking, through the kitchen door, then risked a phone call. Bolly had answered, listened to his strained whisper with very little sympathy, and been no help at all.

"Yeah, all mine are watching me like hawks an'all, Martin. We've got to go to church, haven't we? I've told you, I'll speak to Uncle Les, OK? You're pathetic, honestly."

She had hung up on him, and he had lost his bottle. He did not even dare ring Snatch. Later, when he heard footsteps outside his bedroom door, he had been flat on his back for ages, possibly two hours. His mother had called his name, then come in.

"Good God, whatever are you doing? Don't you want the light on? Don't you feel well?"

Martin could not raise a smile. He moved one hand, dejectedly.

"I dunno. I . . ."

"Oh dear," said his mother, brightly. "Isn't that a pity. We'd better stay in, then."

Martin sat up, abruptly.

"What?"

It came out rather vigorously. His mother eyed him, her head tilted to one side.

"Me and Dad," she said. "We thought we'd pop down the pub for an hour, although it's Sunday. Dad just felt like it and we thought you were on your computer. Never mind."

Martin tried to hide his agitation. At all costs, he must not arouse suspicion.

"No!" he said. "I mean, I don't mind. Of course I don't."

"Well," said Mum. "You could come, too, I suppose. You'd have to sit out, you know what they're like about kids there, but..."

"No, honestly. I'd rather stay. I was just thinking of which game to load, actually. I'm fine."

She was reassured.

"Oh, good. Well, it'll only be for an hour or so, anyway."

Martin, looking much better, feeling much better, had bounced his feet to the floor.

"I've got the number if I need to phone," he said, happily. "You go."

The spring balance came down in a flurry of soot. Martin banged the worst off, then pulled a duster – a torn-up shirt – out of his jeans pocket. He rubbed the soot off, then went very carefully over all the smooth surfaces, as if to polish them. When it went back, there'd be no fingerprints at all.

It was darker, and the stairs were worse than ever. He went down on his backside – how Bolly would have scorned! – clutching the balance in one gloved hand. At the bottom he wiped his sweaty face in the old shirt, then rubbed the brass once more before throwing the duster into the split heart of the staircase. More evidence destroyed. Outside, nothing stirred. The garden was rank-smelling but unfrightening. The alleyway was black but quiet. At the bottom of the high wall, all he could hear close to was his own breathing.

He decided to let it slow down before he went over, but after a minute or so he realised it would not slow down. He rested against the cool brickwork, one palm flat on it, the other on the balance. He studied the bricks above his head, hoping he could climb one-handed without braining himself. At last, knowing he must force himself to go, Martin made a little run at it, the balance tightly under one armpit, and scrabbled upwards. He caught the top with one hand and jerked his left shoulder upwards, jamming the balance with his chest until he could get a proper grip. Then, his feet in good toeholds, he moved his chest upwards, rolling the angular metal, until he was able to trap it with his gloved fingers. A quick wriggle and push, and he was astride the wall. He was panting with exertion now, not fear.

Before that had a chance to return, Martin glanced around the dark and empty yard, changed the position of his legs, and half-jumped, half-slithered to the ground inside. Nothing moved. He was sure the coast was clear, he was even ready not to jump out of his skin if the goat should bleat. But it did not. There was nothing.

Satisfied, Martin ran silently across the yard to the shed where he and Snatch had found the balance. He touched the door handle, gripped it, and turned. The door creaked, not all that loudly, as he pushed it open. Inside, the shed was black as coal. The smell, this time, was not warm and friendly, but full of menace. The small windows let in practically no light, he had no torch, he would never find the place. Standing there, in the aromatic dark, Martin was almost overwhelmed with loneliness.

It was half a minute, maybe more, before he moved. Gradually, as his eyes adjusted to the gloom, he made out shapes. A large store cupboard, a circular saw, a broad workbench, a pile of logs. Martin remembered that the balance had been near the logs, beneath the bench, in a jumble of stuff. Blinking, he moved slowly forwards. There, that was surely it. That was the pile.

When he had almost reached it, one of the dark shapes in front of him moved. As Martin's heart froze in his chest, another shape, to the left of him, became a moving shadow. He opened his mouth, perhaps to scream, but only a small noise came out of it. His fingers opened and the brass spring balance clattered to the floor.

And then a voice said: "Got you!"

A dark, deep, rich West Indian voice. And a light came on, sudden, blinding, and Martin held out his hands in front of him, gloved fingers bent in terror, his mouth stretched open now. Behind him another voice said: "This time, boy – you for it."

His eyes adjusting to the harshness of the light, Martin made out first the older man, the bearded giant, then the shaved-head one. They were smiling at him, terrifying smiles of strong white teeth, like devils in a pantomime. They had both spoken in strange, fearful accents, hardly like English at all. Martin, convulsively, turned to the door, turned to run away.

But beside it, at the light-switch, stood the tall thin youth. His hat was pulled down low, almost to his eyebrows.

"Welcome to the lion den," he said.

# CHAPTER FOURTEEN

For a few moments, Martin's brain raced like an engine. There was nowhere to run to, and no one to hear him scream. He knew he had to say something before the men attacked, but there was nothing to say. He tried to look at them, to put a brave face on it, but he was too frightened. There was still a smile on the broad face of the oldest man, in the split-second that he dared to glance, and it still promised appalling things. He did not move, he was rigid with terror, and he could hear his own breathing, gaspy and uneven.

At last one of them spoke.

"You better come with us. Into the house. We work out our next move."

It was the shaven-headed man, and he still spoke with a

thick accent. He put a hand out to touch Martin, who twitched like a scalded cat. The thin youth pushed the door open.

"Don't try no run. Gate locked. Go that direction."

Outside, Martin gulped in cool, fresh air. He gazed longingly at the high wall that led to home. He could even see his roof. Oh God, he thought. Mum and Dad will be home soon. Oh God.

As the three captors gathered loosely round him, his fear and confusion were almost overwhelming. What would Dad *say*, was the first thought, but it was crowded out by a worse one: would he ever get away to even see him? The wild stories suddenly felt real. He was surrounded by these grim, black men. They could do anything to him. And who would ever know? An empty bed, an empty bedroom, a silent house awaited his mum and dad. How could they track him down?

The youth went ahead of them, and turned the handle noisily to the back door of the house. Martin followed him into a dark lobby, full of the smell of cooking meat. Before the light was switched on he was crowded into the narrow space from behind, cringing in expectation of a blow. It might even be a knife, and his body hunched in anticipation of cold steel. When the light went on, the black men stared at him, as if he had gone mad. The tall youth opened

another door, and heat rushed out. And music.

"Here," said the youth. There was laughter in his voice. "And right on time!"

Martin glanced, glanced again, almost collapsed. The first sensation was shock, then relief, then amazement. Seated at the table, smiling hugely, were his mum and dad. They both had beer in front of them. Their coats were off.

"Mum," he croaked. It was all he could manage. "What?"

"Hallo, Martin," said Dad. "I like the gloves. Computer game still loading, is it?"

The black woman was by the cooker. She was younger than his mother, slim in a blue dress and an apron. She nodded at Martin, her face full of sympathy.

"That's a rotten trick, I tell them. Come in, and say Hello. John, joke over. Everyone."

A trick? A rotten trick? His eyes sought his mother's eyes, and held them. She was completely frank about it, unrepentant.

"Of course it was a put-up job, you fool," she said. "But if you say it wasn't fair, I'll murder you. Come in, don't stand there like a dummy. There's no need to be rude as well, is there?"

Martin's face was blazing. The thin youth – John? – touched his arm, guiding him into the kitchen. The two older men came in as well, but John went past them and back into the yard. He winked at Martin, which only made him blush the more.

"The lady with the pots is Leila," said the shaven-headed man. His voice was no longer thickly accented. He sounded just like black Londoners on TV, he had been putting on an act. He thrust his hand out. "I'm her old man, Ben Starkey, and the real old man there is Joe Raven, Uncle Joe. John outside his son, got it?"

Martin had no choice. He shook the large, black hand. It was very powerful. Then Mr Raven offered his even bigger one.

"Starkey, Raving and Bonkers," he said, his eyes almost disappearing in crinkly skin. "At your service!"

"Mum," said Martin. It was almost a moan.

"You deserve it," she said, briskly. "Sit down before you fall down, love. Cock and bull tales about people finding spring balances by the dyeworks! You must think we're mental!"

Dad pointed to a chair, and Martin took it. Leila Starkey lifted a pot lid and steam gushed out. The cooking smell was rich and spicy.

"What I couldn't get over," said Dad, "was the way you took the bait, Sunshine. Straight in with your eyes wide open, you were such a pushover! Even all that guff about how they'd tear you limb from limb. You lapped it up!"

"They're terrors when they're roused, those West Indians," quoted Mum. "Grrrr!"

"Like bulldogs! Wildmen! And I thought I had a clever son, I thought you're meant to be the smart one!"

"He is a smart one," protested Ben Starkey. "Smart as paint. I am a bulldog when I'm roused, aren't I, Leila! Come on, Jim. Enough teasing. Give the boy a coke."

Martin glanced at his face, and found that he could look at it. It was still ugly, as he had always thought, but it was no longer fearsome. This shaven-headed man was standing up for him, against his parents! Mad.

So was Raven, apparently. His voice was still West Indian, but not like before. He'd been acting monsters, too.

"Maybe Daddy let you have a drop of beer?" he said. "You look like you see a ghost."

Mrs Turner vetoed that.

"He's done enough law-breaking for today, Joe. Give him cola."

Mrs Starkey pointed to a bottle on the sideboard, and the white-haired giant poured.

"How about tea?" he said. "You going to stay and have a bit of tea, Martin?"

Mrs Starkey, straight-faced, said: "Goat curry." Then gave a hoot.

"No!" said Joe Raven. "Leila, you don't mock the boy! Joke over, he had his shock!"

Martin took the glass of coke and nursed it, thoughtfully.

"We didn't mean to steal anything valuable," he said. His voice was small, a little shaky. "It was an accident, in a way. Sort of. I'm sorry."

Ben Starkey was pouring beer.

"It finished now," he said. "Don't worry. It wasn't worth much, and we got it back."

"That's not the point though, is it?" Dad said. "Is it, Martin?"

Martin lowered his eyes.

"No," he said. "I'm sorry. I ... We ..."

Joe Raven came across and ruffled his hair. He felt just

like his father, doing it.

"You had to show the bogeymen," he said. "We understand that. Who's afraid of the Big Bad Wolf?"

"Old Man Quigley used to chase them with a stick," said Dad. "I'd warned him off before."

"It's the excitement, I suppose," said Mum. "You're not a bad boy, are you, Martin?"

"Big Bad Wolf much more exciting," said Raven. "Wolf eat human flesh!"

There was a noise out in the lobby and everybody turned. The door opened, and John Raven's face appeared, topped with his wild hat. Then there was a clattering of hooves and the goat barged in, bleating loudly. It was on a piece of rope.

For a moment, the mad fears rushed back. Martin grabbed his mother's arm.

"You don't...? You won't...? I mean..."

Everyone was watching him. He tried to smile. Of course they wouldn't.

John Raven pushed the goat forward with one hand. It came up to Martin, extraordinarily large. Its eyes were hard and bright, like polished stones.

"She's called Nesta," said the youth. "She's my pet. I've had her since she was a little kid. Stroke her."

Martin gazed. His mind was full of Cy, and Bolly, and

their father's tales. He wished they could have been here for this. Snatch, too. He wondered if he would be allowed to bring them round one day. He could try to frighten them, like he'd been frightened. His dad might cook up some new grand trick for them. He was sure that John would help, he'd ask him soon. John was tickling Nesta's ears.

"She won't eat you, love," his mother said. "There's no need to be afraid."

He was not afraid, of course. He did not bother to explain. He put a hand out and rested it on Nesta's head. Hard, warm and bony. All round him, everybody broke into smiles.

"There!" said Dad, as if he had done something brilliant. "It's amazing what you can learn if you put your mind to it. Isn't it, Sunshine?"

Nesta bleated.